To Izzie and Sebastian, Daisy, Delphina and Johnny, with all my love
—Danie
Et pour Takae, Ferdinand et Natsue, de tout mon coeur
—Danielle

♥

For Cassie Belle,
You're one of my favorite stars.
—Kristi

Text copyright © 2016 by Danielle Steel
Jacket art and interior illustrations copyright © 2016 by Kristi Valiant
Jacket and book design by Jan Gerardi

Visit us on the Web! randomhousekids.com

Educators and librarians, for a variety of teaching tools,
visit us at RHTeachersLibrarians.com

Library of Congress Cataloging-in-Publication Data
Steel, Danielle, author.
Pretty Minnie in Hollywood / by Danielle Steel ; illustrated by Kristi Valiant. — First edition.
pages cm
Summary: "Minnie, a long-haired teacup Chihuahua, travels to Hollywood with her family,
where she gets an unexpected starring role in a movie." — Provided by publisher.
ISBN 978-0-553-53755-0 (trade) — ISBN 978-0-553-53756-7 (lib. bdg.) —
ISBN 978-0-553-53757-4 (ebook)
[1. Chihuahua (Dog breed) — Fiction. 2. Dogs — Fiction. 3. Motion pictures — Production and direction — Fiction.
4. Fashion — Fiction. 5. Hollywood (Los Angeles, Calif.) — Fiction.] I. Valiant, Kristi, illustrator. II. Title.
PZ7.S8143 Pqh [E] — dc23 2015017133

MANUFACTURED IN CHINA
10 9 8 7 6 5 4 3 2
First Edition

DANIELLE STEEL
Pretty Minnie
in HOLLYWOOD

illustrated by Kristi Valiant

Doubleday Books for Young Readers

Minnie is a white, long-haired,
teacup-size Chihuahua.

Minnie belongs to Françoise. They live in Paris.
They love to travel.

One day, Françoise's mother said she was taking her on a trip to Hollywood. She had designed a dress for an actress in a movie. Minnie was sad that Françoise was going away.

But of course there was a ticket for Minnie too!
Minnie even got a brand-new traveling bag.

They were so busy! Minnie and Françoise
had to pick all their outfits for the trip!
And then they were ready to go.

It was all so exciting.
There was so much to
see at the airport . . .

. . . and there was so much
to do on the plane.

Minnie even got to
pick her own movie.

Afterward, Minnie
and Françoise took a nap.

When they woke up, they were
getting ready to land in Los Angeles.

Minnie loves going to hotels.

When they got to their room,
Minnie had a beautiful pink bed.

They went sightseeing that afternoon, and then they came back to the hotel and swam in the pool.

The next day, they took the dress to the actress on the movie set.

Minnie loved meeting all the actors
and eating lunch in the cafeteria.

But then
she met

Fifi.

Fifi growled at Minnie and at the actress.

She was too naughty, so she had to go home.
They needed another dog to star in the movie . . . but *who*?

"Minnie! What about you?"

Françoise told her she would get to wear
pretty clothes if she was in the movie.
That sounded great to Minnie.

The hairstylist made Minnie look extra-fluffy,
and she got her nails done too! Being in a movie
was a lot of fun!

Everybody loved her.
She was a star!

Pretty Minnie
IN HOLLYWOOD
Take 2 | Scene

There was a big party for Minnie and Françoise when the movie was finished. Even Fifi came to say goodbye.

Going to Hollywood was so much fun! But being back home in Paris was best of all.